D0193531

The Adventures of
Wilder Good

#1 *The Elk Hunt: The Adventure Begins*

Lamplighter Finalist 2015–16 (Triple Crown Awards)

"Among the best books for young boys I've seen in years. This is classic Americana, values and all."
—Robert Pratt, *Pratt on Texas*

#2 *Texas Grit*

*Winner of the 2015 Will Rogers Award—
gold medal for "Younger Readers" category*

"I am a big fan of this series. *Texas Grit* is every bit as insightful and positive as the first one."
—Glenn Dromgoole, *Texas Reads*

"Dahlstrom writes about ranch life with flair and specific detail." —*WORLD* magazine

#3 *Wilder and Sunny*

"These are exciting tales . . . Dahlstrom's superb writing takes Wilder through those anxiety-producing years between childhood and adulthood, when life's simplest and most important lessons are learned." —*Forbes*

#4 *The Green Colt*

"*The Green Colt* is told beautifully, with grace and quiet power, and shows S. J. Dahlstrom to be a big new talent. I highly recommend this wonderful book." —Nancy Plain, award-winning author and vice-president of Western Writers of America

#5 *Black Rock Brothers* (coming soon)

THE ADVENTURES OF WILDER GOOD

#1

The Adventures of
Wilder Good

THE ELK HUNT

THE ADVENTURE BEGINS

S. J. DAHLSTROM

Illustrations by Cliff Wilke

PAUL DRY BOOKS
Philadelphia   2013

First Paul Dry Books Edition, 2013

Paul Dry Books, Inc.
Philadelphia, Pennsylvania
www.pauldrybooks.com

Printed in the United States of America

Library of Congress Cataloging-in-Publication Data
Dahlstrom, S. J.
  The elk hunt / S.J. Dahlstrom ; illustrations by Cliff Wilke.
     pages cm — (The adventures of Wilder Good ; [1])
  Summary: As his father helps in his mother's battle with
cancer, twelve-year-old Wilder Good joins his mentor, Gale
Loving, on an elk hunt in Colorado's San Juan Mountains,
where they face threats from fatigue, injury, and a
wilderness predator.
  ISBN 978-1-58988-087-0 (pbk.)
 [1. Hunting—Fiction. 2. Elk—Fiction. 3. Wilderness—
Fiction. 4. Adventure and adventurers—Fiction.
5. Christian life—Fiction. 6. San Juan Mountains (Colo.
and N.M.)—Fiction.] I. Wilke, Cliff, illustrator. II. Title.
  PZ7.D15172Elk 2013
  [Fic]—dc23
                                                    2013019249

for Sören, my beloved

CONTENTS

"But man is not made for defeat," he said. *"A man can be destroyed but not defeated."*

ERNEST HEMINGWAY
The Old Man and the Sea

THE ELK HUNT

THE ADVENTURE BEGINS

CHAPTER ONE
The Old Man

The old man's truck appeared out of the dark, and the rhythmic diesel "slap, slap, slap" made Wilder Good smile. He had barely slept and had been watching from the trailer-house living-room window for half an hour. The 12-year-old boy skipped out of his house quicker than anybody should move at four AM. He carried his backpack and rifle, and wore an ear-to-ear smile.

"You ready, pup?" Gale said from the truck window.

Wilder tried to hide his grin.

"Yeah, I guess. I figured you would over-sleep, old-timer."

"Humphhh. Don't you worry about me."

Wilder opened the truck's rear door and laid his gun and backpack on the seat.

"It's unloaded," he offered.

"Right. Get in, let's go. I think we might get lucky today."

It was early November, and hunting time

was hard to come by. Wilder had begged his way out of a half-day Friday at school to go.

Wilder had barely slept. He always looked forward to those early hours in the truck. They both knew Gale Loving felt the same way, but he wore his gruff countenance as his age seemed to require.

"You bivouac under a pine tree last night?" Gale asked.

"No, but I could've if I'd needed to," Wilder smiled but answered with a slight scowl.

Gale was referring to last winter when they had packed in some hunters horseback to the Weminuche wilderness in the San Juan Mountains. Wilder said he preferred to "bivouac under a pine tree" for the night—only the temperature went down to minus 38 degrees that particular evening. He slept in the wall tent with everybody else. Wilder had picked up the word "bivouac" from reading books by his hero, Teddy Roosevelt.

"Well, it's a good thing we're not packing today. I don't feel strong enough to load you into the back of the truck, just so you can mount Rowdy," Wilder bantered back.

Gale smiled.

Wilder poked at the greasy paper towel bundle that lay on the seat between them. It was hot, like he had figured, so he opened it.

"Mrs. Loving make these?" Wilder asked.

"No, I did." Gale said.

"Yeah . . . right."

Gale's wife, Lucille, had packed them hot egg sandwiches—bacon, two eggs fried over-easy in the bacon grease, and cheese on buttered toast. The kind of food you needed when you were going to hike uphill all day in the mountains.

Lucille must have gotten up at three to make the sandwiches and a thermos of coffee for Gale. Wilder never understood that woman. She was always doing things like this, spoiling Gale and Wilder. Gale called her Lucy, but Wilder always called her Mrs. Loving and smiled when he did it, even though she told him to call her "Cille" like everybody else. Lucille never came on these trips, but she was with them in the truck, just the same.

They drove an hour from town to the trail-head, all the while teasing each other. Wilder and Gale lived in Cottonwood, Colorado, just north of the New Mexico line and right in the foothills between the Front Range and the Great Plains, which stretched from their little town into Kansas and south to Texas. Cottonwood was kind of a border town. One direction, to the west, went straight up to the clouds; to the east, the native grassland didn't stop until the Mississippi River.

They were hunting public land today, and when they arrived there were two other rigs already there. It wasn't like hunting on his grandfather Milam's place off the caprock in West Texas where no one was ever around.

"Watch yourself. There's other guns up here." Wilder knew this, but Gale said it anyway.

They unloaded themselves and their guns in the dark. Wilder wore the backpack his father, Hank, had bought him. It was something he packed and repacked throughout the year, so it was always ready to accompany him at a moment's notice for any adventure—a back-up knife to the one on his belt, matches, various survival items he had never used (candle, compass, emergency space blanket), a water bottle, and a full pound of summer sausage. His dad had raised him on summer sausage in the woods. Wilder's dad wasn't much of a cook, so summer sausage had gotten them a long way together. Wilder also knew from reading the Lewis and Clark journals that pemmican, which was pretty similar to this sausage, was what real explorers ate, and that pleased him.

Instinctively using his hunter's voice, despite still being in the parking lot and in total

darkness, Gale whispered, "Let's go out together until I find where I want you set up."

Wilder nodded and slung Papa Milam's Winchester, still unloaded, onto his shoulder. Gale
had quit hunts on him a time or two before
for that gun infraction, and several other more
subtle violations: walking with your finger on
the trigger, loaded gun in camp—Gale could
be a real crab about gun safety. Referring to
his terse correctives, "It's better than being at a
funeral," he would say.

They walked along seeking to make time,
not stealth. Gale was 72 years old—and it
seemed by the way he had to rock to get out of
his easy chair after watching a Denver Broncos game that he was about done for, legs-wise.
Wilder had learned, however, that those legs,
and eyes, came alive in the woods. Wilder was
no longer handicapped by youth or inexperi-
ence in the woods as he had first been years
ago, but Gale was still his superior in just about
everything out here. This included strength
and endurance. It was just cold enough, in the
mid-20s, for the walk to not make much of a
sweat underneath their clothes. They strode
along in silence, Gale leading. The crisp cold
made their breath smoke.

To Wilder, walking with his old man, rifle
in hand, in the early morning, there was no

greater achievement in the universe. And it was an achievement, not simply something that had happened. He had proved himself in countless small ways that enabled him to get to this point with such a man—safety with a BB gun, a .22, and now a high-powered rifle. The ability to keep up and not complain about weather, hunger, or how much game they saw or didn't. Knowing when to talk and when to shut up and listen around older men. Knowing still that the balance he achieved with his youthful spirit and desire for approval could be overturned at anytime. He was here because he had watched, if not studied, older men. It was a position he treasured, and the anointing he had received by these opportunities was not lost on him.

He might tease the old man, but he revered him.

As the darkness began to fade, they slowed and studied the terrain more closely. Gale felt just about anywhere might be good as any, as there were several hunters in this drainage and they would be banging around moving the elk all over. There was a meadow on a hillside that had good grass before it faded in the aspens on their left about 200 yards ahead. Gale figured that across from there in a thick deadfall would be a good spot. He sent Wilder to find his cover across the little valley. This would put him anywhere from 200 to 350 yards from a shot in the meadow they liked. Gale would go straight up from Wilder's spot to the ridgeline, follow it to the top and come up the drainage from the west at about eleven o'clock. It was seven now.

"Can you handle that?" Gale asked. "I don't want you moving around much."

"Sure. Can you? Don't get lost or die on me up there . . . ," Wilder teased.

"Why don't you let me go?" Wilder asked as the brave but impractical thought hit him. He knew Gale wouldn't let him wander over a ridge alone.

Gale ignored the plea. "If we see one, we'll get him . . . Stay put, pup." The old hunter's eyes twinkled and thinned like knife blades as he gazed down the valley. Then he lumbered off.

Wilder knew Gale's promise wasn't quite as sure a thing as the way he said it—that seeing an elk meant getting him. But he also knew that Gale had killed over 50 elk in his life. He had hunted, guided, and packed in elk since he was a boy, and no one Wilder knew, knew elk and elk country like his old man.

So Wilder found his place and sat down alone in the woods. He had never been good at

51 - Yolo County

being patient, but he would wait and hope, as all hunters do.

Soon it was light enough for Wilder to imagine he could see trophy elk all around. He watched the light invade the dark a few particles at a time, and nothing was as it seemed . . . exactly. Wilder had chosen a nice little setup for himself as he had been taught. His profile was broken up by the hillside and the tangle of deadfall he was in. He sat on a pine log with two larger ones in front of him that he could use for a long-distance rest should he need it. He sure hoped he wouldn't let himself take a 350-yard lob shot at an elk. Chasing a wounded bull around the rest of the day could spoil things. He didn't want to have to tell that story to Gale, Dad, and Papa Milam. A hunter wants to kill quick and clean . . . every time. Taking poor shots and wounding animals gets you kicked out of the club.

He loaded three 150-grain rounds, knowing that he would only get the chance to use one. Hit, miss, or misplace.

He was perched on a finger of woods that overlooked the hillside meadow. The meadow was in the eastern slope of the Colorado Rockies, around 45 miles northwest of Trinidad in the Spanish Peaks area. Concealed by shadow and an army camouflage jacket he had bought at the Salvation Army store, he waited. The camo jacket was not ideal. If he had been wearing something from the Cabela's catalog in a real tree or mossy oak camo pattern, the elk would probably have shown by now. Also, this second-hand (or possibly third) army camo jacket did not meet his personal standards for the consummate outdoorsman image he was trying to develop among his friends. Next year he would have something more appropriate.

Smugly consoling himself, he remembered he was well armed. Wilder carried his grand-father's Winchester model 70. It was a .270 caliber and had 53 years on it in service to Papa Milam. The stock was nicked and dark with years of soaked-in oil. The action was as smooth as glass. Papa had hunted with it all over the West. He lived in West Texas where he had grown up and still ranched on the family place south of Amarillo in the canyon country.

Now 12 years old, Wilder had been given the gun when he turned 11. It was a badge of honor to him. He knew every inch of it from handling it most days after school. He hadn't shot it that much because the ammunition was kept locked up by his dad, but he knew its feel. This was his first real hunt with the rifle. He had used it some already on prairie dogs and jack rabbits, and at the range, blueing his thin shoulder in the process. He was comfortable enough with it now that he would be ready if his old man ever choused an elk through that meadow.

He had changed only one thing about the gun. It had come with Papa Milam's fixed four-power Redfield scope, the black gloss knocked off all the edges. Papa had assured him it worked fine, but Wilder was determined to have a new one. He bought a cheap variable scope that would go from two to ten power. Mounted, it not only made him feel better equipped, but the scope was his own little signature on the rifle.

Gale wasn't an "old man" as most people say it. He wasn't Wilder's father, or grandfather for that matter. His name was Gale Loving. He was an elder at the church the Goods attended. They had started palling around together when Wilder's mother, Livy, got sick.

Livy was fighting breast cancer. It seemed to Wilder his dad spent most of his time taking her to doctor visits and caring for her. That had started five years ago. Livy was thin and frail, and her hair had fallen out and grown back in a few times. But Livy was ranch-raised in drought country, and she had a tender ferocity to her. A lot of that West Texas grit was in her, and she had passed it on to Wilder. They stayed together as a family and did the best they could in the shadow of her illness, which fell over most things in their lives.

It was Gale who helped fill the gap in Wilder's raising. Wilder never thought "Gale" was much of a name for an old man. When they first met, when he was seven, he had said so. He told Gale that never knew a man with that name. His dad had glared at him; Gale had just smiled. Wilder figured Gale never thought much of his name either for he never used it. Wilder was "pup" or the "the pup" when being spoken of, or to.

Like this he sat for the next three hours—glassing with his scope and binocs, figuring the ranges, looking for his lanes. A coyote tempted him sorely around eight-thirty. He was crossing the meadow going wherever coyotes go. Wilder sighted his dog trot in the crosshairs, leading about a foot at 200 yards. And figured confidently he could have had him.

But no elk had come by.

The morning was passing and it was now ten, with no sign of elk or Gale. No shots, no other hunters. Wilder started to worry a little about his old man when this much time got between them. He knew someday Gale would be too old, and there would be no more hunts.

It frustrated him in a childish sort of way . . . that Gale was so old. He always had a math equation running in his head about how many more years he would have with him. "If he lives till he's 80, then we're together till I'm 20. OK, no problem, plenty of time left," he always thought. Running this math problem anew, he caught a little movement.

Something that looked elky was moving in the shadows above the meadow.

CHAPTER TWO
A Hunter's Decision

One of Wilder's immediate problems was that he and Gale hadn't really discussed what to shoot. They both had an either-sex elk tag. That meant they could take the first young cow that came through or, forsaking all else, wait for a chance at a trophy bull. At this point in his life, anything with horns set Wilder's heart pounding.

He also knew that anything with meat, that is, a cow, would help out considerably. He needed to get *something* this year. Like many families Wilder knew, the Goods ate deer and elk year round. It was seldom that they ate out or bought meat from the supermarket.

The shadows moved and grew. There was more than one. Still it was over 400 yards away, and it could be hunters. Wilder raised his gun and peered through the scope, turning it up to full power. He had slid off his hat—a gray Stetson with a cut-down three-inch brim just like the one Papa Milam wore. This one was actually a weather-beaten hand-me-down from him, and he had taught him to use it for a rest. Wilder laid the barrel of his gun down the top crease of the felt cowboy hat, which he then placed on top of the downed tree in front of him. With this rest, Wilder's aim was rock solid.

"Oh boy," he whispered to himself, "that's elk." It was a small herd of seven or eight cows and two bulls. The bulls were a spike and a raghorn bull with a big body. Wilder's breathing picked up, and he felt almost dizzy. They were heading right for the lane he was hoping for, forcing a decision. They weren't spooked, but they were moving. His hands started to shake, and he was scared. Exactly what he had hoped for now seemed a problem he couldn't handle.

The elk were picking their way to his meadow down from the dark green pines and firs, through the first row of fluttering aspens. Hopefully they would stop in his meadow and allow him to calm down, study them, and take his shot. His heart was beating in loud thuds he could feel in his ears and his head. His hands were shaking. It was barely 50 degrees now, but it felt like he was in a sweltering basketball practice back home. Sweat, or the sensation of it, was all over his body.

"Dang it, why am I doing this?" he thought . . . "Relax, pick your spot, and shoot."

This should have been no different than he had done a hundred times with his dad and grandfather on prairie dogs and jack rabbits. But, this *was* different. He was alone with no assuring elder to confirm his shot and target. He had never shot at an elk before, or anything that big on his own.

And he felt pangs of guilt glassing the big beautiful bull elk. Maybe this was wrong and he would be arrested by the game warden if he shot this elk. Maybe God was going to punish him, killing an animal like this just couldn't be right. His courage was fading. Maybe he'd just sit there and let them pass. He laid his gun down.

Wilder wasn't sure he had earned it. And even as he thought that, he wasn't sure what that meant. He just knew that to kill an animal meant *something*. It meant something big. Life was valuable, and he wanted to make sure he respected his game before he killed it. Those who have never hunted would never understand that. But Wilder felt what every hunter has felt—the intimacy and honesty of taking a life for food.

Then he panicked. "Do I even have my license with me?" This was silly of course. He had bought it at Fred's the day they went on sale in September. He had checked and re-checked it a hundred times in the past week, and it had its own special place in a zippered pouch in his backpack. Still, he rested his rifle and mashed around in his pack until he felt the folded paper inside its plastic case. That settled, he glassed the elk again.

Two cows had cautiously moved out into his meadow. He could take either one of them. They were right in his 200-yard zone and the wind was perfect, rising gently out of the canyon into his face and away from the elk. He actually thought for a second he could smell them—musky, raw, hot . . . wild. His setup was just right, as Gale had said, and for one time in a hundred the elk were doing exactly what they were supposed to do.

Now the raghorn was almost in the meadow, and Wilder had decided to shoot him if he presented the right broadside target. He was probably a three-year-old and seemed to have more of a damaged horn than the stunted two-year-old raghorn he had first thought. One side had at least four points, the other just two, and it grew out and up in a strange way. He had been working a wallow and had mud and grass hanging off his horns. He was beautiful, strong. Regardless of the horn size, it was a big, nice bull and would be the first elk Wilder had ever taken.

The crosshairs of the scope, turned up to ten power, rested on the bull now. The animal was huge in the small black window. The world seemed to stop, and all Wilder heard was his breathing, his heartbeat. He attempted to go to that emotionless place you must be in order to kill an animal. His Papa Milam had taught him this one winter calving heifers, but that is another story. Wilder went through his mental checklist again, putting off the shot, unconsciously, fearing the commitment the bullet would set in motion. Wilder wanted to shoot the elk, but just as loudly he wanted to let it pass. Now that the moment he had planned for so long was here, he was not completely sure he had the guts to pull the trigger.

Wilder's mind went through a final list, stalling time, more than being careful.

Hunting license, check.

Hunting season, check.

Gun loaded, check.

Safe shot, check.

Clear backstop, check . . .

About here in his mental progression everything fell apart. As he looked back into his scope, the elk had frozen, stopped their rhythmic chewing, lifted their heads, and were looking behind them. They did this in a spooky, silent unison only wild prey animals can do. Wilder froze too, instinctively, and looked with the elk.

Unaware, Gale was coming up the valley floor in his bright red plaid hunting jacket.

ᘻ

CHAPTER THREE
'Ah, quit carryin' on'

Gale never wore camouflage. Camouflage hunting gear hadn't existed when he was a boy. Despite this lack of technology, he had hunted and killed scores of big game all over his beloved Colorado: mule deer, whitetail, and too many elk to count. He mainly wore clothes made by Filson, which were designed for their toughness during the Gold Rush. Wilder knew the clothes were warm, though Gale actually seemed impervious to temperature. The durability factor was more in Gale's line. As for camouflage—outsmarting the animals was his job, not his jacket's.

Gale was moving just inside the treeline and was very non-camouflaged to the elk, who watched him from half a mile away. He was bobbing along, probably thinking Wilder was asleep or bored . . . anything but moments away from taking his first elk.

Wilder knew he had a precious few seconds to make his decision. The large bull, naturally being the most cautious, had turned up-hill. The cows and spike kept watching Gale, who was moving slowly but now seemed to be coming right at them.

Refocusing on the bull, Wilder confronted a new problem. The elk was now out of position for the broadside shot he wanted. The bull's body was facing directly away from him, slanting uphill with the massive head and neck still turned back toward Gale. The shot was no longer a high-percentage one and had become a more risky spine shot.

A few of the cows moved, and Wilder knew they were about to bolt. Gale was a quarter-mile away now. Wilder was mad and defiant, both at himself and the deteriorating situation. The bull made a step and lowered his head. The crosshairs steadied on the middle of his back . . . and Wilder pulled the trigger.

Boom! The gunshot exploded across the canyon and into the meadow.

The .270 bucked into Wilder's shoulder, and smoke rose from the barrel as he quickly chambered a new round. That follow-up chambering of a fresh round was automatic. Many times he did it twice as he never remembered the first follow-up. He would open the chamber a second time and, to his surprise, discard a fresh, unfired round.

He had taken the shot more to ease the tension than from having convinced himself it was the right shot. Instead of the elation at a good hit, Wilder felt a sucker punch grow in his belly.

The bull was hit. Wilder knew that, even though he hadn't seen the impact. The recoil of the .270 was still a little much for a 120-pound body, and he hadn't been able to keep his eye in the scope through the shot. He looked up quickly, though, and saw the bull hump up and run up the hill. The cows went crashing with him willy-nilly as they raced in retreat, gaining altitude. Spooked elk seemed to hit every deadfall, rock slide, and brush pile as they plowed their way toward safety. Wilder listened until they topped the ridge, and then the mountains went silent again.

Wilder knew this was bad. He had not made a vital hit. His only real shot from that angle was the spine shot, and a solid impact there would have crippled the elk and laid him down immediately. His grandfather Good back East shot deer this way, and Wilder had seen him do it many times. Wilder glanced at where Gale had frozen and was swinging his gun into position behind some aspen saplings. He was crouched, looking in Wilder's direction, patient and alert.

Once the elk had topped the ridge and spilled over, Wilder figured it was OK to move. He waited for eye contact with Gale again and stood up. When Gale saw him, he stood too, feeling and trusting that any suspense was over. They met in the green winter grass at the bottom of the drainage.

"What did you shoot, pup?" Gale began.

"A nice raghorn bull. I got nervous when you showed up and made a bad shot."

"He's hit?"

"Yes."

Wilder swore.

"I knew I shouldn't have shot. I'm sorry." Slapping his leg, he looked off. Wilder was careful to use the cowboy cussing that had crept into his language sort of muffled, under his breath, as if Gale wouldn't notice.

"Ah, quit carryin' on." Gale mused. "And don't swear. Homer wrote the *Iliad* and *Odyssey* without using that language. God tried to drown the human race without saying it."

They both mused a second or two at the little swear word speech, Gale tickled with himself.

Gale getting onto him stunned Wilder for a second.

"Where's he hit?" Gale continued.

"I did everything wrong. I shot when he

was facing away from me up the hill. They spooked when you came up, and I got jumpy."

"Yeah, I figured that, but where do you think he is hit?"

"I don't know . . . " Wilder was embarrassed. He was living out his worst nightmare for the hunt. He had wanted so feverishly to prove himself—even though he knew he didn't need to.

"Well, let's go check for blood," Gale said.

They began to move toward the meadow. Wilder felt sheepish. The spring in his step that was so strong earlier was gone now. Gale wasn't upset, but he wasn't offering any motivational speeches either. If a 12-year-old wanted to wallow around in self-pity, he would let him. Wilder would have to learn this.

They searched the meadow and right off found blood, a lot of it. It was thick and red and wet. It smelled stronger than deer blood and mixed with the high, clear air and the pine scent. Gale and Wilder both smiled. There was hope. The bullet had definitely hit the elk hard in either the upper back or flank. Clearly if it hit a flank, no bones had been broken. The best case was that it hit the elk in the upper back and took out some secondary organs, possibly even getting into the lungs.

The blood trail led right up the drainage,

where Wilder had watched the herd disappear. The ridge topped out after 250 yards of fairly steep deadfall pine forest. Gale was thinking about their plan. The top of the ridge was still in the treeline and looked thick.

"Your bull is hit hard, and he hasn't seen or smelled what hit him. If he topped that ridge like you say he did, he's going to sit up there and catch his breath. And if he's hit hard enough, he's going to lie down."

"And if he's not hit hard . . . ?"

"If your bullet is in his leg muscle, he's three miles away by now and the coyotes and magpies will eat him next week."

"Yeah, that sucks." Wilder slapped his leg again.

"Don't say that, either."

"So what do we do now?" Wilder countered.

"We eat," Gale said, with a smile.

They took off their packs and propped their rifles on an available deadfall bench in the meadow. The weather was nice now, 50 degrees and rising, and clear. Wilder pulled out his considerable hunk of summer sausage and cut it up for the two of them with his hunting knife. He also had some now-broken crackers and cheese. He cut this up, too. They drank from their water bottles. Late in November now, the elk had quit bugling for the most part. As they sat in the bright winter grass, patches of crusty snow dotting the meadow from an early storm, they heard a lone, raspy bull bugling from miles away. Like a vicious cold front, its call seemed to bounce back and forth up the drainage, hitting them in the face and continuing on.

Soon they would be tracking Wilder's bull up and over the mountain.

ᘺ

CHAPTER FOUR
The Stalk

After their meal, Gale lay back on the grass. He was in no rush. But Wilder was up and arranging his pack and triple-checking his gun.

"When are we going?" he asked. All his youthful smart-alecky attacks on Gale had faded into a quiet bashful obedience. It was awkward for both of them. Their constant badgering of each other was where they were most comfortable.

"Calm down, pup. We want that elk to sit down and forget about us . . . and hopefully die."

Wilder stewed.

"Well, I just don't want you to start snoring after that gourmet meal. That won't help us either." Wilder tried to relieve his nervousness, but knew he sounded stupid and immature now. His stomach ached.

"Hummph," Gale acknowledged. He was thoughtfully chewing a toothpick, which stuck out from his grizzly, whiskered mouth. He could always produce a toothpick, even deep in the mountains.

They lazed around in the warm midday sun, the kind that always feels like it's happening for the first time when you're high up in the mountains. A pair of gray jays showed up and picked boldly at their lunch leavings. Wilder liked them and teased the brave, seemingly irritable little birds with sticks as they darted in and out snagging crumbs.

Gale eventually got Wilder talking about his favorite subject, the Denver Broncos, but Wilder wasn't particularly interested in discussing football at that moment—not to mention his team was the Dallas Cowboys. Gale sat and thought, relaxed, careless, and comfortable in the mountains—as if he had been in the easy chair in his living room watching the Broncos on TV. Wilder could think of nothing but his wounded bull. He knew he was on the precipice of bagging his first elk or facing the disappointment at wounding such a beautiful animal and having him get away.

"You about ready to go find your elk?" Gale said finally, as if the thought had just hit him and Wilder had been causing the holdup.

Wilder jumped to his feet. "Of course I am."

Gale checked around to make sure they had all their gear. A cracker wrapper and

Gale's handkerchief were the last items on the ground. Gale still carried a handkerchief all the time, something that made Wilder a little queasy whenever he saw it.

As they prepared to move out, Gale made a little speech.

"OK, this might get a little hairy. If that bull is up there hit hard, he is going to be bedded down somewhere where he can see us before we see him. He'll likely still have plenty of juice in him, and he'll bolt, fast, when he sees us. We need to be ready. If we don't get him then, we will never see him again. We'll have to take a running shot if that's all we get. When we get close to the top of the ridge, have your gun chambered, with the safety on. Keep your finger off the trigger—just like quail hunting. And shoot till he drops."

Wilder nodded in silence, eyes fixed on the old man, unblinking.

"Of course, he may be dead or long gone," Gale threw in as they began their creep uphill.

They followed the bloody trail straight up through some nasty-looking deadfall snags. Blood was smeared across the tops of bare pine logs where the bull's belly had dragged like a big, sloppy paint brush. Halfway up, the re-treating band of elk had hit a game trail that angled them towards the top. Wilder and his

old man took the same trail, and it made their
approach to the top easier, and better yet, qui-
eter. The pines were thick and hadn't been
burned in a long time. You could get glimpses
that went 100 yards, but actual shooting visibility was closer to 40 yards, and that was
still thick. The years of pine needle mulch beneath their feet on the trail kept them quiet as
the Utes and Arapahoes who had hunted these
trails years before in their moccasins. Or so
Wilder figured. He often fantasized about In-
dians and couldn't help but do so now as he
snuck through the timber.

They neared the crest of the ridge. They
could see that the narrow game trail was going
to ease up and over it. A perfect setup, they
both thought in silence, making eye contact
one last time. The blood sign was fainter now,
but still visible. Wilder was ready, but he gladly
let Gale go ahead. He stayed close, knowing he
had the green light to shoot as well. They were
right at the top and almost to eye level where
the sloping rise would allow them to begin to
see onto the down slope. Ready to make their
stalk, Gale turned to Wilder and nodded for
him to take the lead.

Wilder's heart pounded afresh. "Oh God,"
he thought. It was an exclamation more than a
prayer, which bothered his conscience. He felt

his heart might beat out of his shirt. He knew he couldn't argue now; talking was obviously out of the question. He swallowed, looked back at Gale with wide eyes and then just sort of froze. Gale motioned again. Wilder took a step and forced himself to do what was expected of him. "Don't blow this, don't blow this," he told himself. Gale smiled quickly but avoided eye contact, trying to make it seem natural. Not knowing any other options, Wilder moved into the lead.

Wilder chambered a round in complete silence, the way you can only do with an old, slick, and worn action. His gun was ready— he knew that, no problem there. He had killed dozens of quail in this same manner: slow stalk, gun down, then a rush and a quick shot—safety on and his finger in the flag position as he had been taught.

Why did quail hunting seem so mild and this elk hunt so terrifying?

The top of the ridge leveled out, and they began a slow descent down into some other forgotten drainage of the eastern slope. It faced northwest, and the sun was bright in their eyes. The pines were sparser on this side and visibility was better. It was clear that it had been burned in the last ten years, but the fire had stopped on the ridgeline. Gale pointed

Wilder to stay on the ridge and look deep into the pines beneath them. Wilder raised the binoculars that hung at his neck. Seventy yards in front of him, the woods opened up a bit, and a mound of deadfall sat like a stack of bleached dinosaur bones. Snow patches and winter grass highlighted the immediate edges.

Behind one of the base logs of the interweave, a funny looking branch was sticking out. It contrasted a dark brown with the bleached and bare straight pine limbs. As Wilder gave it a second look, the branch turned toward him ... and it had eyes and ears.

〰

CHAPTER FIVE
'Shoot, Wilder, shoot'

Gale had predicted it correctly. With no time to think, Wilder reacted, dropping to one knee. The bull rose with a casual, dignified immediacy as all elk do, even when surprised. Dropping the binocs, Wilder had his gun up by the time the bull was. A long red streak ran from the elk's back down his side, belly, and leg. He couldn't run directly away because the log pile blocked his route. This gave Wilder at least ten feet along which the bull would have to move broadside to get clear of the pile. He had his window.

Wilder's finger was on the trigger, his thumb flicking off the safety. The elk did an about face and was taking off. But Wilder could not find him in the scope; everything was blurry. He had forgotten to turn it down from ten power! His heart sank as he eased his head back and forth on the stock trying to get a full, clear circle and sight something that looked furry. All he got were partial black circles and timber. He could not shoot.

"Shoot, Wilder, shoot!" Gale whispered, now standing at his side.

Wilder didn't look back, but looked up again to check the elk's position: two more long strides and he would be gone. It had only been four seconds since they laid eyes on each other. Wilder took the elk's bearing and peered through his scope again, finger on the trigger. His heart was pounding again, out of excitement and, now, anger. There was no time to adjust the scope. He had to find that elk and squeeze a shot off.

He thought he caught a glimpse of brown hair and began to tighten his finger . . .

Boom!

The shot came from his side. The brown patch he was about to squeeze on vanished. From his kneeling position, he lowered his gun and looked up and over, shocked and wide-eyed. Gale was smiling, toothpick still in his wide grin, as he lowered his gun and chambered a new round.

Glancing down at Wilder he said, "Get on him, pup!"

Shaking off the momentary trance that Gale's shot had caused, Wilder quickly saw that the elk was down and struggling. Wilder immediately turned down his scope and found the bull. He was still down, but he wasn't still. His head was up, and then his front legs pawed the wet pine floor.

"Finish him Wilder, now!" Gale said this with great emotion. While he had killed game big and small in the thousands, the suffering of any of them touched a place that was near the surface in the old man. This was especially true for these mighty elk that he had lived with and hunted for so many years of his life. The elk was hurt and definitely going to die, but Gale wanted Wilder to slam the door shut as quickly as possible.

Wilder's aim was ready, and he squeezed the trigger almost the moment Gale told him to. His .270 roared, and the elk lay flat. It was over.

Gale seemed unmoved by the sudden drama. The relief of the tension, however, made Wilder feel light-headed. He sat down.

"We got him, pup!" Gale exclaimed as he slapped the sitting Wilder on the back. "Just like I told you."

"Yeah, we . . . did," Wilder said slowly. A smile began to spread across his face, and the realization washed over him.

"Yeah, we did," he repeated as he melted into the mountain and lay on his back.

"Let's go take a look at him."

Wilder got up, and in unison they both checked that they had chambered fresh rounds. They put their guns on safety and stalked quietly but directly, and soon covered the ground between themselves and the elk. It was with awe that Wilder approached the bull. He lay still, a hulking mass of Colorado wilderness. Assured he was dead by their proximity and noise, and by Gale's lack of caution, Wilder went straight to his horns.

"Wow, Gale, he's bigger than I thought! He's a good one isn't he?"

"Yes . . . yes, he is a nice bull. Not really a raghorn like you said. A five by four. He had a little harem of cows this year and had fought off a slew of younger bulls. Probably his first year to really fight. And look at the broken brow tine. He was a fighter."

"How old do you think he is?"

"At least three, maybe four. He's a good bull, pup."

Wilder beamed as they recounted the hunt step by step, replaying everything, taking their time over each detail. They said everything they possibly could about it, the stalk, the shots, the weather, relishing each moment while it was fresh and new. Wilder didn't bring up his failure to shoot; neither did Gale. They both figured it was a mistake Wilder wouldn't make again. Wilder knew he would be looking for his grandfather's old Redfield scope when he got home. But he also knew Gale was proud of him and he had taken the lead, and that was enough.

But, as Wilder was about to learn, the real work of elk hunting had just begun.

CHAPTER SIX

The Real Work
of Elk Hunting

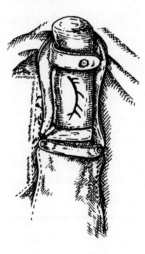

They took a few pictures with Wilder's camera and then turned toward the elk with a workman's mindset. They now had to get the elk to the truck. Because they hadn't brought horses on this trip and they had no four-wheeler, they would bone the meat out and carry it themselves. The good thing was they were only four miles or so from the trailhead and it was mostly downhill.

Gale pulled his knife out from a leather sheath on his hip. Gale's knife was a wonder to Wilder. It had been given to Gale by a blacksmith in Montana when he was younger in exchange for some horse work. It was carbon steel, which meant the five-inch skinning blade was black from use, not shiny like the cheap stainless-steel knives Wilder owned. It had a bone handle with a small turquoise inlay design—a delicate, seven-point elk antler, tiny and beautiful and blue. The light blue turquoise gave it a refined, elegant look. Wilder knew the knife had made quick work of hundreds of game animals and moved like an extension of Gale's hand in the bloody work of field dressing.

Wilder unsheathed his knife too and stood there with it in his hand.

"Is your knife sharp, pup?" Gale asked, but more implied.

Wilder nodded and understood this was his direction to lead the process. He had no problem with this since he had done several deer on his own and watched many more. However, he was a little nervous at the sheer bulk of the 800-pound elk in front of him. They had rolled him onto his back with his head uphill, Gale puffing like a freight train tugging on the antlers. The elk was so heavy it felt like he was glued to the ground.

Gale got in position to keep the elk's rear legs spread apart and allow Wilder some room to work.

The way to learn such things, Wilder had observed, was to charge in and figure it out as he went. Mistakes would be forgiven; cowardice was not. Wilder had long ago learned not to expect Gale or any other man to give him step-by-step directions. The way to get something done was simply to keep trying, allowing his errors to be his guide. A direct question would be answered ... maybe ... but he couldn't count on it. His dad's favorite saying, it seemed, was "Just figure it out."

Like his camouflage, Wilder's knife was not his ideal. It was a cheap, plastic-handled blade he had purchased at a pawn shop. It did say "Winchester" on it, but he knew it was made in China because of the stamp on the other side. He had tried to file the "China" off. It was unreadable now, but the scratches testified to its origin. This annoyed Wilder. His dad had taught him to shave a bit of his arm hair to judge a blade's readiness. He didn't have much arm hair to begin with, so there were always bare patches on both arms, more on the left as he was right-handed. He wished he had a knife like Gale's, but the one he had was sharp, for now at least.

Wilder began the cut by finding the elk's breast bone. Poking delicately through the thick hide and matted hair, Wilder smelled the first whiffs of hot body-cavity blood, offset lightly by the airy pines. He loved this smell. Partly because he had developed an appreciation for it out of necessity. He was exposed to it often and had made up his mind not to be grossed out by it.

There was another reason he liked the smell. Somehow, it seemed holy. Like the sacrifices and burnt offerings Wilder knew about from the Old Testament. It reminded him of the smell of burnt calf hair at a branding. There were few people these days who ever smelled such things. If you were smelling this mix of blood and heat, then you were in an inner circle of men. These were wild aromas, far from the schoolroom, church building, or city. Like a secret handshake, these smells meant you were among a higher class. Men who were the best men Wilder knew. The kind of man he wanted, and intended, to be.

Wilder made his way down the belly with his knife, making the crucial, careful cut between the skin and the elk's bulging, thin-walled paunch—a paunch that contained gallons of putrid rotting grass and stomach acid, which would spoil a fair share of meat and make their job unpleasant if he punctured it. He didn't. (He had done that before.)

Towering above the boy, Gale watched closely and was pleased.

Wilder had gotten the elk unzipped and worked with his knife and a rock to split the pelvis. A hatchet would have been better for this, but he got it busted and began spilling out the hot mess of entrails onto the forest floor. Gale just grunted now and then as Wilder finished each of the minor tasks in the process, messy but competent. Wilder had his sleeves rolled up now, as the mountain temperature was warming. Blood was up to his elbows. He didn't cut up from the breastbone much. He wanted to keep the head and cape intact as much as possible, although he knew he didn't have the money for taxidermy—much less a place to put such a huge head. It felt good to have to think about such things as if he had killed a real trophy, and had the money to mount it and a wall sufficient to hang it.

Gale noticed his carefulness, but said nothing. His eyes just twinkled at his young protégé.

Wilder cleaned out the inside—liver, lungs, windpipe, and the massive elk heart. Gale helped him, rolling the huge carcass back and forth between them. It was a process that would have been easier had the elk been positioned a little more upright, or better yet, been hung in a tree, but that was a luxury only a horse or a pickup's strength could have provided.

Wilder paused, out of breath, and stood up with his bloody hands on his hips. He toed the heart with his boot.

"You want that heart for Ernesto?" he asked. Ernesto worked for Gale on occasion in Gale's construction business. Ernesto ate a lot of parts they didn't.

"Naw, leave it. We'll have our hands full with the meat as it is. Plus you'll be wanting to drag out that head, I figure."

It seemed strange to Wilder that the head was an afterthought to Gale.

Wilder let Gale cut out the long red backstraps. He worked quickly, like he was filleting a fish, and wasted none of the smooth tender muscle. Wilder bagged these and laid them on a clean, flat rock. Gale took off the hindquarters and, one at a time, they hung them up for de-boning in the nearest pine. They each weighed over a hundred pounds, and it took Gale and Wilder's best efforts to keep them out of the dirt. They had been working an hour now, so they took a break to stretch their backs. Each took a long drink from his water bottle. Wilder was using his backup knife now and he made some strokes on the little pocket whetstone, spitting on it first.

They had worked in a comfortable silence and now rested that way, too.

"Let's finish up," Gale said after five minutes, just as the first sweat had begun to crust on their foreheads.

Wilder knew what that meant. It was past one-thirty now, and they had at least one, probably two big hikes in front of them. They set back to work as if they were in a factory, busy and watching the time. Neither wanted to be stuck up here in the dark.

Wilder separated the front shoulders, and they had all four quarters hanging. Wilder held the meat bags, and Gale filled them carefully, cutting and shaving the red, bulky muscles into roast-sized chunks. Wilder placed each bag on a big lichen-covered rock. Gray jays and a lone magpie had discovered the kill and were darting in and out picking at the carcass.

The meat was quickly bagged. Wilder marveled at the efficiency of Gale's blade. Compared to his own jagged, probing knife work, Gale's work was fluid and deliberate.

"How many elk have you cut up?"

"Oh, probably hundreds, including deer," Gale replied. "One time in Wyoming when I was young, we had a bunch of elk trapped in an old buffalo wallow that had become a cottonwood grove. We were all poor and knew we needed to shoot a bunch of them. My buddy and I shot 20 or more and then got the neighbors. I guess that was when I really figured it out. I took no pleasure in it. We were butchers, not hunters. We tagged and dressed all of them and spent the next two days straight, cutting meat."

"Wow."

"Don't ever shoot 20 elk, Wilder. Times were different then. We had to. There were some families who depended on elk. That's all they had." The meat bags and Wilder's head, horns, and cape sat before them. The cape looked like a big wet blanket and must have weighed 70 pounds. Wilder wanted to get his head out first and started tying it to his pack. It was already a little after two o'clock.

"Leave the head. We need to get the meat out first."

"Yeah, I guess you're right."

"Tie it and the cape high up in the tree to keep the birds and coyotes off them."

Wilder did this with the rope Gale had used to hang the meat, tossing it high over a branch and tying it off to the tree trunk—a job easier said than done, Wilder found out. He glanced up, sad, thinking he might never see it again. He was proud of that head.

Gale stuffed 60 or so pounds of the bagged elk meat into his pack and helped Wilder load about half that. There seemed to be an equal amount still lying on the rock. That plus the head wouldn't work. They reloaded a bit more and stared at their packs which lay like bloated ticks on the grass. They knew that once they shouldered them the hike would begin. The pair set themselves mentally for the task by sipping water neither needed. With luck, they should be back in three hours, they figured.

With a grunt Gale swung his pack up and onto his back. Wilder harnessed himself into his while it still lay on the ground. Then he rolled over like a turtle to get under the weight and did kind of a pushup to get his legs under him. Wobbling, he closed his eyes and pushed up with his legs. It was more weight than he had ever carried before. His heart felt weak and his gut hurt with anxiety. He wasn't sure he could do this. Gale watched from the corner of his eye, careful that Wilder didn't see him watching, not wanting to give him the opportunity to let his fear turn into a whimper for mercy.

"Let's go. Four miles is nothing."

"Yeah. I hope you don't have a stroke. I can't drag you and my bull out of here."

"Ha, pup. You'll be lucky if the coyotes don't start trailing you."

Wilder had proved himself in many ways to the old hunter, but carrying this much weight for four miles would be a new test. Not sure how this would go, the old man led off down the trail.

CHAPTER SEVEN
Hurt

Wilder and Gale killed their elk on a ridge that rose 400 feet above the trail that lay in the valley below. They immediately had to retrace this moderate slope, up which they had tracked their wounded elk. The bloody elk steaks felt like liquid and seemed to slosh around on Wilder's back. Standing still with this 40-pound load was enough, walking with it made each step an adventure in whether or not he was going to keep his stick-like legs under him. Going downhill made this proposition even more of a joke.

He had loaded plenty of 50-pound sacks of cow cake for his grandfather on the ranch. But having one strapped to your back was something else altogether. He felt the load was driving him, not the other way around.

Wilder only weighed 120 pounds, a fact he bemoaned every time the school nurse or a doctor checked him. He wasn't sure when the puberty deal was supposed to start either.

He'd heard so many rumors. At some point he expected to sprout muscles and begin shaving. He had the vague idea that it would just *happen* some morning and he would wake up as a stocky 200-pounder with a dark, whiskered face.

Puberty wasn't a subject he would bring up with Gale.

For now he was trudging downhill, stepping sideways using the whole mass of each boot to steady himself, just hoping to make it. This descent didn't force him to breathe hard, but the constant muscle tension was already making his back and legs ache terribly. They were about halfway down and had to cross the same deadfall area they had crossed before, with no easy way through or around it. He and Gale had almost skipped across these logs on the way up, in silent, unburdened pursuit of the bull. He hadn't noticed the dangerous latticework of the fallen pines to be quite so treacherous then.

Wilder placed each foot carefully, balancing himself with branches that stuck up from the barkless deadfalls, where he could find them. Not only was he going downhill with all that elk weight high on his body, but now he was standing three feet off the ground, still at that dreadful angle. Going up the mountain, he would have had a short fall to the ground;

heading down the mountain, a fall could be dangerous. When he could, he straddled the downed tree trunks and sat while he pulled his second leg over.

Taking a step downhill, his foot snagged for a moment on the tree he was trying to step over. In that instant of hesitation, he placed his foot too far behind the top-heavy weight that was now hurtling him toward the ground of the downhill slope. He couldn't get the foot under him in time. Knowing he was going down, and badly, he pulled his foot free and pivoted so as to land backpack first on the tangle of deadfalls in front of him. His precious rifle banged roughly into the trees. The sharp, dried, broken pine branches stuck upward waiting for him like spear points.

Gale turned at the sound of the crash. The snapping of assorted bone-dry pine twigs and branches was loud. Wilder never hollered, and instead of rolling to a stop, hit with a thud onto the trees . . . and seemed to stick. Gale dropped his pack and rushed over. Wilder looked up and smiled, ashamed, and faintly but surely searching for mercy.

"Are you hurt, son?" A tenderness crept in as Gale accidentally replaced "pup" with "son." Neither mentioned it, but both noticed.

"Umm . . . I'm sorry, Gale."

"Sorry for what? Can you get up?"

"I think so."

Wilder struggled up after unbuckling his pack and left it where it fell. He was bleeding in several places on his arms and face from the sharp branches. Still in a daze, he steadied his feet and stretched. That's when he felt a sharp pain in his calf, and he looked down.

"Ouch!" Wilder saw the blood running down his leg. "What's that?"

Gale saw it too, as Wilder sat down on the tree. Gale rolled up the pant leg and looked closely. A snag had punctured and ripped his pant leg and then the skin at the top of his calf as he had spun and crashed. There was a nasty two-inch gash—more of a puncture. Gray pine dust floated in the blood and sides of the wound from the pine dagger. The pain sunk in, and Wilder cringed.

"That's a good one, son," Gale said, "How deep did it go?"

"I don't know."

"Can you flex the muscle?"

Wilder flexed the calf up and down. There was a deep pain. He grimaced and hopped a little circle on the other foot.

"I think it is all right."

"Yeah, right," Gale said smiling, "but . . . I'll need to doctor that a bit. Stop the bleeding, clean and bandage it."

"I'm sorry, Gale. My foot caught and I couldn't stop myself."

"I know, Wilder. I put too much on you."

"No, I can make it."

Gale fumbled through his pack. The kit was underneath 60 pounds of meat. He had given himself too much as well. In his mind, he let go of making two trips before dark. They would be slower now, much slower. And that was if Wilder could tough it out.

Gale knelt at Wilder's leg. The boy had his boot and sock off, and Gale flushed the wound by squeezing his water bottle all around it. The blood mixed with the water and ran down Wilder's leg, making it look worse than it was. Gale knew this, but it made his heart race, panicking a little in his mind. He wasn't given to cursing out loud, but his mind returned to France in 1944. There was plenty of swearing then. He had bandaged a lot of friends.

The iodine and hydrogen peroxide made Wilder wince and jump a bit. Gale broke out the silver packets of blood-clotting powder.

They were uncannily similar to the stuff he had used 50 years ago. He sprinkled the powder on the bloody gash and it immediately did its job.

Wilder just sat there, brave like he had been taught—unaware of the thoughts of his nurse, who was caring for him with old, experienced hands. Gale packed and wrapped the leg tight.

"I wrapped you a little tight. Can you stand it?"

"Yes, it's fine," Wilder said without thinking. Gale figured he would have said "yes" if his leg was cut off. He had always admired the boy's grit, but now he feared he might have trusted it too much.

"We have to make sure that bleeding stops, which will be hard with us walking. I'll reset it as soon as you need it."

"I'm fine, really," Wilder said optimistically. "Patch us up and get back to work."

"Yeah, I guess. If you are going to be dumb, you've got to be tough," Gale mumbled to himself.

That was one of Gale's standard lines to Wilder, although this time he meant it for himself. He had put too much weight on their packs. It stung more because he wasn't the one bearing the pain of his bad decision. Wilder seemed so much bigger most of the time; Gale sometimes forgot he was still a young boy.

"We'd better get going, son."

"I'm ready, old-timer."

〰

CHAPTER EIGHT
Little Boy

When he had reloaded his pack, Gale made Wilder a staff. The dried pine stick was hard as a baseball bat, yet light. Wilder found his gun. Plenty of new scratches in the stock, but it had been unloaded, of course, and safe in the fall.

Wilder didn't yet know how difficult the walk was going to be. Gale did. Carefully they continued their descent. Wilder could bear the pain—the muscle seemed untouched . . . well, maybe nicked, and he knew he was bleeding under the still bright white bandage. The tightness of the wrap felt good and actually made him feel stronger than before, if only for a while.

They worked their way down slowly, eager to reach the relatively flat floor of the valley. The day's heat had broken by the time they sat on a deadfall on the level ground. The mid-afternoon mountain stillness broke with a rush of cool air that carried the smell of a coming heavy dew. The wet aroma also cut a little as both knew they would not have time now to come back tonight.

"Gale, we'll have to leave my head up here all night, huh?" Wilder said.

"Yes, it looks that way. We don't have a choice. And we're not back to the truck yet with this load either."

"I tied it high in that spruce—nothing should mess with it . . . right?"

"Well, nothing eats antlers that I know of, except porcupines. And it would take an awful ambitious one to eat all your horns in one night. We'll be back tomorrow to get it."

That made Wilder feel better. Gale wouldn't lie to him.

"You don't think a lion or bear might find it?" Wilder queried further.

"Sure, either of those scamps could come across it or our gut pile. Whoever finds the gut pile and the rest of the meat will have a full meal of that first. You'd have to be real unlucky to have a cat or bear eat all that and then climb the tree to mess with the other."

"I hope I don't lose that head."

"I know. How does your leg feel? Do I need to tighten the bandage, or change it?"

"No, I'm fine. Let's get out of here."

Wilder turned and stomped off down the

trail, naively, forcing himself to act brave. He hoped Gale would follow without making him look back over his shoulder. Wilder listened as Gale rose and lumbered after him as he had hoped.

It was three miles now to the truck. The first muscle ache set in quickly. Adrenaline must have gotten him down the mountain because he had felt little from his body then. Now the wet feed sack of elk meat strapped to his back felt like an anchor trying to drown him. The trail rose and fell gently and wound its way through the thick grass meadows and boulders of the drainage. Water ran here and there making its way down in pools and bogs and then disappearing into a subterranean cavity, only to show up again 30 yards down the trail. The bogs were pungent and still held their share of bugs and mosquitoes even though it was late in the year. Wilder's Gore-Tex boots kept him fairly dry. But the mud made an evil suction with each step that further wore on him.

Wilder marveled to himself how easy the walk in had been. How each light step they had made up the valley was now a grueling effort back the other way. How could it all be so different now? he thought.

Fear grew at the realization that he might not be able to make it. The sun was about ten minutes from the western peaks, so they would have light for another hour. Wilder began to doubt himself.

He felt the way he had the first time he hauled hay with Papa Milam in West Texas. The alfalfa bales weighed about the same as his pack did now, and they had been fun to lift and load at first. Being in the field at sunup with the fresh cut hay and his grandfather and two hired hands felt right. It had been 70 degrees, and they had eaten burritos and were joking and talking. That was at seven AM. Two hours later, Wilder had wanted to curl up in a ball and die. He had never been so exhausted in all his life. The truck was going too fast to load, the bales had gotten heavier, and he had a headache. The pitiful looks he gave his grandfather hadn't made any difference. Finally he had asked to steer the pickup, which was steering itself just fine, driverless, up till then. Watching his grandfather and the other men work gave him a bad feeling. Exhaustion had made him a coward. He had given in that day, and didn't want to feel that way again.

So he trudged on down the mountainside, perhaps wishing for an excuse to quit walking, but refusing to make one up. It was the honesty from the hay field that drove him on.

A few minutes later, the sun was down, and

the cool mountain passage hung in the elusive beauty of dusk. Just like at dawn, when he had sat and waited for the elk that was now strapped to his back, nothing was quite as it appeared in the half-light. All seemed either beautiful or threatening, but both were illusions. Maybe a mile and a half still lay before them.

"Let's take a sit, pup," Gale ordered as they passed a convenient rock ledge that rose on the side of the trail. They sat and swung their packs off in unison.

"Yeah, I'm dead."

"How is your leg?"

As if he had forgotten it, with the burden of the backpack taking most of his mental complaints, he glanced down.

"Oh yeah, uhh . . . it's fine . . . I guess."

Wilder wasn't trying to sound tough, he had just overlooked that problem in the pain and worry about his bubbling cowardice.

"Let me look at it and repack it. We have one last leg of the trail, and then we'll be out," Gale said. "We may have to do the last bit in the dark."

"Patch me up, doc. But it feels fine." Wilder tried to sound optimistic, which they both knew was a lie. "My pack is killing me, though."

"You'll make it." Gale offered no options.

Gale lifted Wilder's leg. They saw the saturated bandage and knew it was still bleeding. After soaking through the white bandage, the blood had begun a bright red drip line into Wilder's sock.

"Geez," Gale thought to himself, "I hope I don't kill this kid." The fear and doubt he felt never trickled out, however. They never had, and Gale didn't have to practice keeping them in. They never surfaced, ever.

"You're leaking pup. It doesn't hurt though, huh?"

"Not really. Do you think it'll need sewing up tonight . . . when we get back?"

"Oh yeah, definitely. The clinic in town will be open, and we'll get you in there—if for nothing else but antibiotics."

Gale repacked the gash in Wilder's calf. He pulled the bandage tighter this time. Wilder's skinny white leg looked so small in Gale's weathered aged hands, which were still tinted red with elk blood. The boy's calf muscle was meager, but it was sinewy and tough. Gale loved that about him, and without that toughness, there would have been little to endear a 72-year-old man to a 12-year-old not his kin.

They had to get out tonight, and there was nothing for it. Gale would be watching Wilder closely from now on, for loss of blood and shock. If he swayed or weakened, they would ditch the meat. In the very end, Gale knew and prepared himself, he might have to carry the boy out.

The wound re-bandaged, they moved off together into the coming darkness.

CHAPTER NINE
Being Stalked

The walking stick proved to be an excellent idea, and it got plenty of use in the half-light. Wilder worked it like a blind man, carefully finding footing for it with each step as if it had been a third foot that needed watching. Gale let Wilder lead so he wouldn't feel pushed. The oncoming darkness made things difficult, but the trail was easy to follow, and the night would not be cold. They just needed to take their time, and they would get out safely.

Wilder daydreamed about the sound of his pack landing in the empty steel pickup bed, about sitting in the safe, cushioned seat, and mostly . . . about the ice-cold Dr. Pepper he knew waited for him in the cooler. "Oh boy, cold Dr. Pepper." That thought pushed him on.

Wilder threw one of his thousand-pound feet atop the rock that leveled onto the path to the right of creek. He noticed for the first time how bloody his boots had gotten cleaning the elk—and that they now had some of his own blood on them, too. He smiled and thought of his secret girlfriend, Sunny.

She was in seventh grade with him. He adored her and had since kindergarten. She had glowing, sun-bleached blond hair that blew in the wind when they played kickball and when she arched her head back and giggled with all her might on the swings. She had a petite little nose that had slowly grown tiny brown freckles every year since he had known her. He touched that nose once by accident while playing basketball. He stared at her in class and memorized her expressions, her movements. He wrote her little poems he kept secret like—'*Her hair is fair like the mountain air.*' She was a magic he couldn't explain.

He knew he would marry her someday.

But her dad was pretty strict about boyfriends and girlfriends and such, so those were words they never used, but they both knew. At least he was pretty sure she knew too.

He thought of her now when he saw his boot because yesterday, as he bragged about missing school for the elk hunt, she had told him, "Get some elk blood on your boots." She was that kind of girl, beautiful and sweet, but she had been raised in the outdoors by her dad . . . full of hunting and fishing and cows and horses. Sometimes it stressed Wilder just to keep up with her. But she would love to see his boots come Monday at school, he was sure of that.

He also noticed that thinking of Sunny seemed to make the pain go away . . .

The trail crossed the boggy creek-bed drainage again and rose a little on the other side. It continued under an eroded rock wall that shot up hundreds of feet over their heads. As Gale glanced up into the blue-toned half-light, something heavy moved on that wall. It moved quick and quiet.

Gale considered what it might be. He knew it wasn't elk—those rocks would have made noise as the animals spooked and scrambled off, and there would have been more than one. It could have been a lone mule deer, but at that angle up out of the canyon, he probably would have seen the antlers or big ears sky-lined. Another hunter watching the trail from that rock ledge made sense. But he would have hollered at them, not hidden himself and moved like that.

Gale trusted his eyes. They were old but sharp, and a lifetime of watching game movement and wild places had honed them to a fine edge. He didn't have to see exactly; he could feel the landscape around him. He was no interloper. He was just as much a part of his surroundings as the rocks and trees and the spring that his feet stood in now.

It was that sense that told him—a mountain lion watched them.

The bottom of the drainage was a tangle of willow shoots and elderberry thickets. The trail stayed high on rocky soil looking down into the bottom. The rock face loomed high over their heads, as the trail wound downward along the mountain, in and out along the wall. They couldn't see much to their sides, only front and back. Adding to their natural blindness because of the geography, the sun was down now. But the trail glowed, being well worn, in the subtle three-quarters moonlight.

If it *was* a cat, he would be hunting them now. They had been moving like a pair of mule deer, right down the trail at dusk, as the big feline would have surmised. Their smell was thick with blood—100 pounds of fresh elk and a hemorrhaging teenage boy.

Gale gently grabbed Wilder's shoulder from behind.

"Time to take a break. Almost home."

"Huh?" Wilder replied, as if coming out of a trance. His mind at the same time wandering, but also focused on the trail.

"Take a break," Gale repeated.

Wilder wiggled a shoulder to drop his pack.

"No, keep it on. What shape is your gun in?"

Wilder slung it off his shoulder, knowing already, but checking.

"Loaded, nothing chambered, safety on. Why? You feeling jealous and want to shoot another elk tonight before we get back?" Wilder smiled. Their competition and good-natured antagonism was still hearty, despite the circumstances.

"Recheck it."

"What for?" Wilder asked as he complied, sliding his bolt open and fingering the chamber with his pinky in the dark and then carefully closing the bolt while holding the full magazine of cartridges down.

"No elk, son. I think I saw a cat on the ridge back there, and he moved down in our direction. Right now we look and smell pretty good to him. And it would seem we are in his ambush zone in this drainage."

"A cat?" Wilder was puzzled.

"A mountain lion, could be a big one."

"Oh." The statement and possible danger didn't quite register with Wilder; his mind was moving slowly with fatigue and exhaustion.

"I want you to walk behind me, close. Sling your rifle on your back again, and promise me not to chamber a round or shoot at anything unless I tell you to . . . Are you listening to me, Wilder?"

"Yeah, sure. Don't shoot a mountain lion."

"Put on your headlamp. He already sees us perfectly. Our lamps might serve to blind him or mess with his eyes a bit. They might scare him off, too."

Wilder fumbled around in the side pocket of his Army jacket for the headlamp. He found it and put it on. Gale knew Wilder was not all there right now. He wasn't in shock, and he hadn't lost a dangerous amount of blood, but Gale knew they were close to their limits. They just had to go another half-mile and they would be safe. Another half-mile, he thought, gritting his teeth.

Wilder understood the situation more than Gale knew—a mountain lion hunting you at night was dangerous. Nevertheless, he was more amused by it than scared. It wasn't courage, simply exhaustion. He was in that place where any distraction from the weight on his back and the pain in his leg was welcome. Wilder almost *hoped* to see the mountain lion. It would be a good addition to the day's adventure. He never really considered that it was an animal that could kill him, or kill Gale and leave him stranded on the mountain.

"OK, let's go. And watch out," Gale started.

They could recognize the trail now, and knew a few more bends would put them at the trailhead and the salvation of the pickup truck. Contrary to his order to Wilder, Gale's .270 was loaded and its round black barrel broke the darkness in front of them with each step.

Starting with a low growl that crescendoed into a high, terrifying other-worldly pitch, the cat screamed.

CHAPTER TEN

'That was something'

If Wilder had been only partially cognizant of the situation before, he was fully alive to it now. The scream stopped his heart. He was terrified. He froze behind Gale.

Gale turned to his right as the scream seemed to come like an avalanche of hot, hateful air from a crag in the rock face 20 feet above them. His headlamp's beam shot over as he pivoted, providing blessed light, but also leaving pitch blackness everywhere the beam wasn't hitting.

The shaft of light swiveled over with Gale's head . . . no cat. Then his beam angled up, probing the night and the rock wall. The light found its subject where the sound seemed to have blasted out into the night.

Twenty feet above their heads, a tan, mature lion was crouched to spring. Gale's beam formed a circle around him—cool yellow eyes in the middle.

Wilder was still frozen facing forward, heart

pounding, but he looked over and in his peripheral vision saw the huge cat. The impersonal lion eyes stared right at him. He was fully lit by Gale's headlamp, every feature bright and clear. The cat seemed like a stuffed mount or a zoo exhibit—so close, yet so real.

Gale's rifle had swiveled with his headlamp. The .270 was trained on the cat and the safety switched off instantly by the old man. Gale didn't want to shoot if he didn't have to. A wounded cat would be much worse, and a one-shot kill shot would be unlikely, even at 20 feet.

Gale had been plotting various scenarios as they walked—thinking ahead about what and how he might have to do things. In the three seconds the cat stared at them, undoubtedly surprised and blinded by their lights, Gale made his move.

"Heeyaaahhh CAT! Get out of here!" he screamed as loud as he could while shifting his feet and keeping the barrel trained on the middle of the beautiful yellowish-tan hide.

The cat appeared to squint as if turning up his binocular power for a better look. His muscles re-tightened, and new ripples appeared on his shoulders.

Gale's finger made contact and applied some pressure to the four-pound, custom-tuned trigger. And he hollered again, "YAAAW cat, move on!"

In the instant of Gale's second yell, as if he had been splashed with a bucket of cold water, the cat realized that they weren't deer. He jumped straight up from his crouched position, reversed in mid-air, and disappeared from the cone-shaped window that the lamp made in the night. They listened in dark silence and heard him bound off up the escarpment of rock and gravel. Heavy foot pads touching rock with force, little quiet thuds, but still perceptible.

In the ten seconds it took for this drama to play out, Wilder had not moved a muscle. The adrenaline worked quickly, and there was no pain in his shoulders or the gashed leg. Then he relaxed his knotted muscles and opened and shut his eyes several times with big stretching full-face blinks. He shook his head side-to-side, closing his eyes. Opening them, he found Gale's headlamp on his face, the old man smiling.

"That was something, huh, pup . . . Wow!" Gale beamed.

"Uhh, yeah, that was something," Wilder stammered. "Did that actually just happen?"

"Yes, it did . . . Wow." Gale was caught in the moment. "That was something. He was beautiful.

"Yeah . . . Wow," Gale kept mumbling to himself.

"What do we do now?" Wilder whispered, thinking they should be quiet or cautious or something.

"Yeah, you're right . . . let's get out of this drainage," Gale said.

Gale started walking. Wilder didn't have to be told to stay close. He alternated looking to the side of the trail with his headlamp and then back to the trail and his old man so as not to trip. It was risky to look up every few feet, but he really couldn't help watching for the lion.

Gale saw the beam flashing up the mountainside.

"That cat is gone, Wilder. They either decide to fight or run off," Gale deadpanned, ". . . unless they don't."

"Yeah, unless they don't," Wilder deadpanned back.

"Anyway, he won't scream a second time. He would just jump on your back and clamp down on your neck. You really wouldn't feel a thing," Gale chuckled.

"That doesn't scare me. Hugh Glass fought a grizzle bear and lived. That cat would probably jump on you, anyway." Wilder paused. "Predators kill the old and the fat and the weak first. Everybody knows that."

Wilder chuckled out loud, amused with himself. Gale just made a "humph" sound.

Wilder was belligerent in his exhaustion now, "It's called survival of the fattest . . . I mean fittest."

CHAPTER 11
Tell Me Your Adventure

Wilder and the old man kept up the banter for the last half-mile to the pickup. When they got there and their packs made a dead thud in the truck bed, Wilder tilted the icy-cold Dr. Pepper as the big diesel engine rumbled, loud and comforting. Thirty seconds later, Wilder was asleep, and Gale drove the 50 miles into Cottonwood in the dark and in silence.

The doctor at the clinic flushed Wilder's wound, which should have been painful to the exhausted boy but somehow wasn't. He quickly put in five stitches, and they were done. Neither Gale nor Wilder thought to call Livy and Hank at home, but the nurse did. When Gale dropped Wilder off around midnight, Livy was up, waiting. Her frame was delicate, and Wilder could feel her backbone as they hugged. As they embraced he said, "I got an elk Mama." She smiled, and a tear fell onto his camo jacket. Wilder slept until ten the next morning.

He might have slept later, but his little sister, Molly, jumped in bed with him when she woke around eight. She snuggled in next to her big brother and, since it was Saturday, slept hard again under his warm blankets. Molly was four years younger and had slept in the same big bed with Wilder when she was little. She had big brown eyes and long brown hair and thought of Wilder as a superhero. She always loved the chance to be close to him—especially when he was still.

But eventually she woke again and lay staring at the ceiling. Her quiet stirring woke Wilder.

"Get out of here, Flopsy," Wilder said half-heartedly. He called Molly "Flopsy" after Peter Rabbit's little sister.

"I'm being quiet. You smell like elk."

Wilder smiled with his eyes closed. "Yeah, I do," he thought.

"Did Gale bust one?" Molly pushed for answers.

"You don't talk like a girl. Bust one..." Wilder laughed.

"Well, did he?"

"No."

"Well, why do you smell like elk, and I've already found that big bandage on your leg. What happened? Tell me!"

"Oh, nothing big." Wilder was enjoying

it now. He knew how to play the nonchalant hero well. But Molly was ready for this.

"I'll tell you who called for you—if you tell me your adventure."

"Who called!?!" Wilder jumped, surprised.

"Tell me first what happened in the mountains."

So that's what he did. He slowly told her the entire day, like a good big brother. Livy listened from the hallway as brother and sister lay in bed talking back and forth. Wilder acted slyly disappointed when Molly told him that Sunny had called last night. Molly said it was just about homework and that Sunny had said the teacher "made her call." Wilder smiled knowing, and hoping, different.

"Momma's going to Denver next week for doctor stuff. You're going to Papa's the whole time." Molly stated.

"Really?"

"Yup, it's for something important. I'm staying with Cille."

They were both used to the trips to Denver and knew to put a good face on it. That was their life now, and they all did the best they could. Wilder stared and thought of his grandfather's place. He was always a little anxious, because he knew there would be work there, cow work. But the cow work was a thrill, even though Papa Milam was hard and tough. He would probably get a chance to deer hunt, too.

Finally, as Wilder lay there, he remembered he had to get the meat and the elk head out of the mountains. He got up and asked his mom where Dad was. She said he had gone with Gale early that morning to get the rest of the elk.

So Gale and Hank hiked up to Wilder's elk that morning at sunup and retrieved the head and cape. Coyotes had been into the meat. When they got back to town, Gale took the mount to Whiskey Don, the taxidermist he used. Don's hands were arthritic, big knots and curls like mesquite roots, and nobody knew how he did such good work. He said he didn't think he could do it for under 500 dollars, and everyone in town knew Wilder's family didn't have that kind of money. Gale just told him to do it and he'd be back to pick it up in the spring. Whiskey Don knew what that meant. The pup had earned it.

THE END

ABOUT THE AUTHOR

S. J. Dahlstrom lives and writes in West Texas with his wife and children. A fifth-generation Texan, S. J. has spent his life "bouncing around" the countryside from New Mexico and Texas, north to Colorado and Montana, and east to Michigan and New York. He is interested in all things outdoors and creative. He writes poetry and hunts deer; he plants wildflowers and breaks horses; he reads Ernest Hemingway and Emily Dickinson and C. S. Lewis.

S. J.'s writing draws on his experiences as a cowboy, husband, father—and as a founder of the Whetstone Boys Ranch in Mountain View, Missouri. He says, "I wrote this story about Wilder Good for kids who grew up in the outdoors and for kids who long for the outdoors . . . working, fishing, hunting; farms, ranches, mountains and prairies. I think all kids want to do these things and go to these places." He has numerous magazine credits for his writing and photography. THE ADVENTURES OF WILDER GOOD is his first book series.

You can learn more about S. J. Dahlstrom and join Wilder Good on his adventures when you visit the Wilder Good website, *www.WilderGood.com*, where S. J. encourages readers to 'Be Wilder' and submit photos and stories about their own adventures.

The next Adventure of Wilder Good:

#2 **Texas Grit**

The Adventure Continues

#2

THE ADVENTURES OF
WILDER GOOD

TEXAS GRIT

NOV 0 3 2017

CPSIA information can be obtained
at www.ICGtesting.com
Printed in the USA
LVOW12s0908270117
522394LV00001B/1/P

9 781589 880870